THE
ANIMAL
WORLD

of

Thornton Burgess

Illustrated by HARRISON CADY

PLATT & MUNK, Publishers

NEW YORK

CONTENTS

LIBRARY OF CONGRESS CATALOG CARD NUMBER: 61-8463

FLASH, THE YOUNG DEER

Young Flash felt quite grownup. He was nearly as big as his father, Lightfoot the Deer, and was wearing his first crown of real horns. Long, long ago the last spot had disappeared from his coat.

"Only babies wear spotted coats," he scornfully told Jumper the Hare when Jumper admired the coats of Flash's small brother and sister.

He was no longer a fawn, and he wanted everybody to know it. Had not mother, busy with the care of the twins, sent him out to find a place for himself in the Great World? Best of all he had his first set of horns. My, my, how proud he was of them. All summer they had been growing. Flash

spent much time admiring them in his reflection in the still water of Paddy the Beaver's pond. At first they had been soft and tender and he had had to be very careful of them. They were hard now, real weapons with which to fight anyone his own size. Yes, Flash felt quite grownup.

Reddy Fox crossed his path. When Flash was younger he had feared Reddy. Now he snorted, lowered his head so as to present the sharp points of those horns, pawed the ground with a fore foot and dashed at Reddy. Reddy merely leaped aside and grinned as Flash dashed past. When Flash turned Reddy had disappeared in the bushes.

Head held high and white tail up Flash proudly made his way to the pond of Paddy the Beaver. But he was too smart to allow pride to overcome caution. Before stepping out in the open he carefully peered out from a place where he could see all of Paddy's pond and the surrounding shore. There on the farther shore stood his father, Lightfoot the Deer. Flash was sure that nowhere else in all the Great World was a deer so handsome. His beautiful head was crowned with great antlers carrying ten points. It was held high. He looked startled yet unafraid as he started toward the end of Paddy's dam. Flash looked that way. There, standing upright like a man, was great big Buster Bear. A little shiver of excitement ran all over Flash. What was going to happen?

He didn't have to wait long to find out. Crack! Over near the shore half way between Lightfoot and Buster, and unseen by either, Paddy the Beaver had been floating. He had lifted that big broad tail of his as high as he could and brought it down on the water, kerslap. It made a report like a gun. Lightfoot leaped into the air, turned and with

HARRISON CADY

high bounds disappeared among the trees. Buster Bear dropped to all fours and lumbered off in the other direction. Flash whirled and bounded away. I suspect that Paddy the Beaver grinned, but of course I don't know.

In a few minutes Flash realized what had frightened him

so. He stopped running. He came to an old wood road. It led to an abandoned lumber camp. He remembered that over in that clearing he had found a big stump, around which he had found delicious salt. It had been put there for deer by fishermen, who were camping in one of the log buildings. They knew that deer will travel miles and miles to find salt. It is one thing they seem to crave most and never get enough of.

An old doe, Flash's grandma, had driven him away before he had time for more than a lick or two. Twice since the same thing had happened. Perhaps today she wouldn't be there.

Flash stood just where the road left the woods. Grandma was there. There was bitter disappointment in his eyes. Beyond the old doe, his mother and the twins, in their pretty spotted coats, were quietly feeding. An idea popped into Flash's head. With a whistle as of alarm he bounded out into the clearing, running as only a badly frightened Deer can run.

Grandma didn't wait to see what the danger might be. Away she bounded, her white flag, as a Deer's tail is called,

straight up. Mother didn't stop to see what the danger might
be. Off she bounded, her white flag up. At her heels
bounded the twins, their little white flags up. In a jiffy all
had disappeared in the woods.

Flash stopped running. He walked over to the stump and
began licking salt. Every few seconds he would lift his head
to listen and to look over toward the woods where the others
had vanished. By and by Grandma appeared. She was
cautiously stealing back, looking for the cause of her fright
and to see if the way was now clear.

When she saw Flash at that salt she forgot everything
else. Hadn't she three times warned him to keep away
from there? Out of the woods straight at Flash dashed
Grandma. She reared high to strike him with her sharp-
edged hoofs. Flash was watching and ready. He jumped
aside and raced back up the old road. Grandma chased

him a little way, then returned and began feeding around the old stump. Mother and the twins did not return.

Flash kept out of sight up the road. After a while Grandma got over her nervousness. Mrs. Grouse came out from the woods and began to pick about near the big, old doe. They were old friends, those two. At last Grandma was facing straight away from where Flash was hiding. Her head was down as she nibbled grass. This was what Flash had been waiting for.

A crash in the brush back of them, and the sound of feet galloping as in fright, sent Mrs. Grouse whirring off in one direction and the big doe, leaping over logs and brush in headlong flight, in another direction to get out of sight among the trees.

Once more Flash had the salt to himself. This time Grandma did not return. When at last Flash was satisfied and started back to the pond of Paddy the Beaver for a drink, I fear he strutted a little. You know young people who do smart things sometimes do strut. They shouldn't, but they do. And I think you will agree with me that Flash really had been smart to fool his wise old Grandma.